Yzma

Kronk

Kuzco the Lama

A catalogue record for this book is available from the British Library

Published by Ladybird Books Ltd
27 Wrights Lane London W8 5TZ
A Penguin Company

2 4 6 8 10 9 7 5 3 1

LADYBIRD and the device of a Ladybird are
trademarks of Ladybird Books Ltd

© Disney MMI

DISNEY'S

THE EMPEROR'S

NEW GROOVE

Ladybird

Emperor Kuzco was having a good day!
He'd shouted at the peasants for no
reason, and fired Yzma, his Royal Advisor.
Then Kuzco called for Pacha, a town
leader from the other side of the jungle.

"When I give the word, your little town
will be… bye-bye!" said the emperor.
He proudly showed Pacha a model of his
summer home, Kuzcotopia, which he
wanted to build on top of Pacha's town.

Pacha begged Kuzco to change his mind. "But where will we live?" Pacha asked.

"Hmm... don't know, don't care!" said the emperor, and he told Pacha to get out!

Yzma was furious that she had been fired and so she decided to poison Kuzco. In her laboratory under the palace, she found a deadly potion!

But Yzma's helper Kronk, who wasn't very clever, picked up the wrong potion – and poured extract of llama into Kuzco's glass by mistake!

Growing longer ears, fur and hooves, Kuzco suddenly changed into a llama.

"Hit him on the head, take him out of town and finish the job!" ordered Yzma. Kronk did as he as told – well, almost...

Kronk put the emperor in a sack and threw him into the canal. But Kronk felt very guilty, and pulled the sack back out!

As Kronk wondered what to do with the emperor he tripped and fell down some stairs. The sack flew out of Kronk's hands and landed on a cart – Pacha's cart.

Pacha didn't notice the sack land onto his cart, and he began his long journey home. Kronk watched as Pacha left the city with the emperor. Yzma wasn't going to be happy about this!

When Pacha got home, he found the sack and opened it…

Kuzco poked his head out and Pacha went to stroke the llama's head.

"No touchy!" yelled Kuzco

"Aaaahh! Demon llama!" yelled Pacha.

"Where?" said Kuzco. "Wait a minute, I know you – you're that peasant!"

"Emperor Kuzco?" said Pacha.

Kuzco ordered Pacha to take him back to the city.

"I can't let you go back unless you change your mind and build your summer home somewhere else," said Pacha.

"I don't make deals with peasants!" hissed the emperor. And he set off into the jungle alone.

As Kuzco wandered through the jungle he met a friendly squirrel named Bucky, who offered him an acorn.

"Hit the road, Bucky!" snapped the emperor, rudely.

But just then Kuzco slipped and rolled down a hill. When he landed at the bottom, Kuzco looked round him. He had landed in the middle of a pack of jaguars!

Kuzco started to run but the jaguars could run faster than the llama. The jaguars chased Kuzco to the edge of a steep cliff. But just as Kuzco thought it was the end, Pacha swung down on a vine and rescued him.

Back at the palace, Kronk was
behaving strangely.

"Kuzco *is* dead, right? Tell me
he's dead," said Yzma.

"Well, not as dead as *we* would
have hoped," said Kronk.

"We must find him then!" screeched
Yzma, when Kronk explained
what had happened.

As Yzma and Kronk headed for
Pacha's village they met Bucky,
who told Kronk where he had
seen the llama.

Yzma and Kronk followed
the llama's trail to a
jungle restaurant.

Pacha and Kuzco had stopped at the restaurant for some food. Llamas weren't allowed inside, so Kuzco was disguised as a lady!

Kuzco was being difficult as usual and went to complain about the food, just as Yzma and Kronk sat down at a table nearby. Pacha overheard them talking…

"I should have done away with Kuzco myself when I had the chance!" said Yzma.

As Pacha went to warn Kuzco, Kronk looked over at him – the peasant looked familiar.

But when Pacha told Kuzco what he had heard, the emperor didn't believe him.

Kuzco pushed Pacha away and walked over to join Yzma and Kronk. But he heard Yzma tell Kronk, "We must track that llama down and finish him off for good!"

Kuzco now realised that Pacha was his only friend and he went to find him.

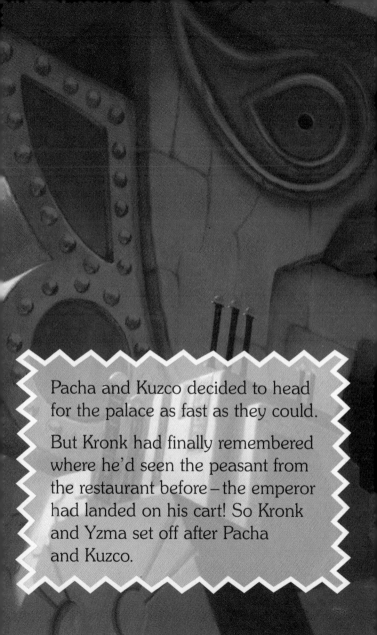

Pacha and Kuzco decided to head for the palace as fast as they could.

But Kronk had finally remembered where he'd seen the peasant from the restaurant before – the emperor had landed on his cart! So Kronk and Yzma set off after Pacha and Kuzco.

Reaching the palace, Kuzco searched Yzma's laboratory.

"Looking for this?" said Yzma, stepping out of the shadows. She had got there before them! Yzma was holding the potion that the emperor needed to become human again.

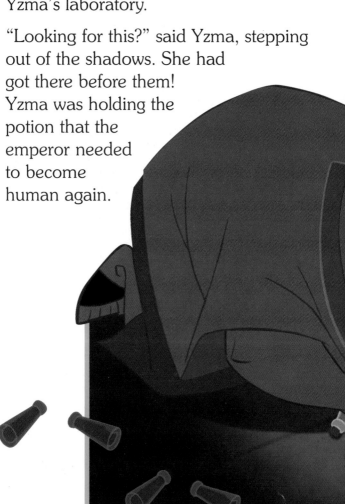

Leaping forward, Kuzco tried to grab the potion, but it landed amongst dozens of other potions that had been knocked over!

Suddenly, the palace guards burst
into the laboratory and attacked them.
Pacha and Kuzco threw the potions at the
guards. As the potions hit them, the guards
changed into lizards, cows, and even
an octopus!

"Run, Kuzco!" called Pacha, scooping up the few remaining potions.

As the two friends escaped, Kuzco kept trying different potions. First he turned into a turtle, then a bird, then a whale – and then back to a llama!

Soon there were only two potions left.

Yzma, who had followed them, tried to grab the potions from Kuzco. But she lost her balance and fell onto one of the potions which changed her into a cute little cat!

That just left one potion, and that was how Kuzco got the potion that changed him back to a human.

After all the excitement of the last few days, Kuzco decided to take a holiday in Pacha's village. He even built a little hut next to Pacha's.

"We had some fun together, didn't we!" smiled Kuzco.

"We sure did," said Pacha.

At last, as he sat with his new friend, the emperor realised that he didn't need to build Kuzcotopia. He could enjoy Pacha's village just the way it was.

Kuzco

Pacha